JOE-JOE NUT AND BISCUIT BILL ADVENTURES
CASE # 1: THE GREAT PIE CATASTROPHE

JOE-JOE NUT AND BISCUIT BILL ADVENTURES

CASE #1:

THE GREAT PIE CATASTROPHE

RENÉE HAND

NORTH STAR PRESS OF ST. CLOUD, INC.

St. Cloud, Minnesota

ISBN-10: 0-87839-351-X
ISBN-13: 978-0-87839-351-0

First Editon: March 2010

Printed in the United States of America.

Published by:
North Star Press of St. Cloud, Inc.
P.O. Box 451
St. Cloud, Minnesota 56302

northstarpress.com

Dedication

Thank you to Joe Wojtowicz, Jr., for giving me the idea for Joe-Joe Nut. I would also like to thank the biscuit brothers, Mark and Ted Bienkowski, for always making me laugh throughout the years. This one is for all of you. As always, thank you to my family and my boys, Gabriel and Sheldon, for inspiring me every day.

CONTENTS

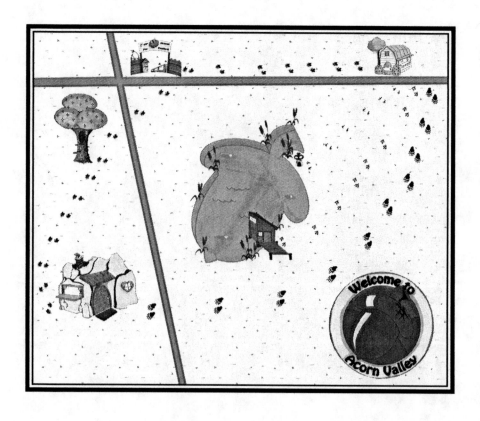

1

THE MISSING PIE

At Acorn Valley Elementary, Biscuit Bill the duck and Joe-Joe Nut the squirrel, the best animal detectives in the valley, were helping first and second graders make pies for the forty-second annual pie festival. The students wanted to sell them as a fundraiser so they could take a field trip to Moose Falls. Biscuit was a great baker. His mother was a gourmet pastry chef and had her own bakery on Thirty-second Street. She had taught him everything he needed to know about cakes, pies, and all sorts of desserts.

Joe-Joe, on the other hand, was much less experienced in the kitchen. He was more of an eater, rather than a baker of pies. In fact, Mrs. Doolittle, the second grade teacher, kept peering her black-and-white cow face over his shoulder correcting him on his choice of ingredients and his methods.

It wasn't until the end, after Joe-Joe's pies had exploded and leaked all over the oven for the second time, that Biscuit decided it was time to leave. By then, Joe-Joe's hair and clothes were covered in flour and the cherry filling he had made. Joe-Joe had worn an apron, of course, but it seemed that the flour and filling had landed everywhere else *except* the apron.

The teachers and students thanked both Joe-Joe and Biscuit for taking the time to help with their fundraiser. Biscuit of course, received most of the thanks, for his pies had turned out the best and added a dozen to the class count, while Joe-Joe's two explosive pies had to be thrown away and the oven and the counter and the floor and, yes, the ceiling washed.

After they left, the pair walked swiftly to their white van in the parking lot. Biscuit

unlocked the back doors, and he and Joe-Joe hopped in, changing to their uniforms in record time. Gone were the casual clothes they had baked in. Now they wore their flashy black detective suits that they were known for. Of course, not all the flour or cherry filling could be gotten out of Joe-Joe's fur, but he rubbed and brushed out as much as he could. Once finished they both climbed into the front seat. Within minutes, Biscuit was driving away from the school heading towards the main road that led them back into Acorn Valley.

The day was sunny and bright. They both put their sunglasses on. Joe-Joe was so wiped out from their morning assignment, that he couldn't resist lowering his seat back to get more comfortable. He propped his feet on the dashboard and tucked his hands behind his head. Before he knew it, he was fast asleep. Ten minutes later, Joe-Joe woke to the sound of their police radio going off. Though his nap was short, he felt rested. He quickly sat up and wiped the drool that had been flowing down his chin on his sleeve, then watched Biscuit reach up towards the

dashboard and press the button. Dispatch was calling them.

"Biscuit Bill here," Biscuit said in his most official voice.

"There's a problem at Miss Cluck's residence," Dispatch told him. "It's something about a missing pie? You might want to check it out. Miss Cluck lives at 102 Old MacDonald Lane."

"We'll do, Dispatch," replied Biscuit.

Joe-Joe began to laugh as he glanced into his sun visor mirror and saw the flour in his hair and a red glob of cherry filling at the top of one ear. He quickly lowered the window, stuck his head out and shook. He then brought his head back into the van and glanced again at the mirror. His hair was standing straight up. He looked like a porcupine with a spike, but the flour and cherry filling were gone. Joe-Joe ran his hands through his thick red fur trying to get the hairs to lie down.

Biscuit laughed loudly and shook his head. "Enjoy your nap?"

"All that baking really wiped me out," replied Joe-Joe.

"You really need to come over and take cooking lessons from my mother again," said Biscuit.

"I know, but the last time she kicked me out of her kitchen and said not to come back," replied Joe-Joe.

"Well, you did catch her kitchen on fire," Biscuit reminded him.

Joe-Joe smiled and shrugged sheepishly. "I did apologize for that," he said still smoothing his hair.

"Out of curiosity, do you cook at all when you're home?" asked Biscuit.

"Not unless I have too. Unlike your mother, mine wasn't much of a cooker or a baker. Mine was more of a gatherer. You should see the mess I have in my kitchen. I still haven't found a way to repair my ceiling after the last time I cooked."

After a few minutes of laughing, Biscuits features and tone became more serious. "Don't you cook your food?"

"That's what the microwave is for. Well, *was* for. Did you know that you shouldn't put metal anything in a microwave?"

Biscuit Bill was speechless, his mouth open in shock. After several minutes, he was finally able to speak. "Joe-Joe, that's rule number one. No metal *ever* goes in the microwave. Never mind, this weekend I'll come over and give you some tips, okay? I'll even help you fix your ceiling. That's what friends are for, but now we need to focus on our next case. We have a mystery to solve."

Biscuit turned down a few streets and made their way over to Miss Cluck's. The scenery was beautiful. Flowers of all different colors bloomed wildly and the trees swayed back and forth in a gentle breeze.

Miss Cluck lived in a white house with blue shudders. Flowers and bushes were tastefully planted around the foundation, making the landscape quite appealing. She seemed to be particularly fond of the color blue. Before Joe-Joe got out of the car, he made sure he grabbed his notepad and pencil. Then he joined Biscuit, who was already standing in front of the door. Before they could even knock, the door swung open. Miss Cluck was in a frantic state, losing feathers

as she flapped her wings around and ran in circles.

"Miss Cluck," began Biscuit. "My name is Biscuit Bill and this is my partner, Joe-Joe Nut. We're detectives, and we're here because of a missing pie. Could you tell us more about it please?"

Miss Cluck tried to calm down and invited Joe-Joe and Biscuit to enter.

"My pie! My pie!" clucked Miss Cluck, feathers flying again.

"Now, ma'am, we're here to help you. You must calm down and tell us what happened from the very beginning."

Miss Cluck took several deep breaths. Her eyes closed briefly as she tried to calm herself. Joe-Joe and Biscuit waited patiently. When Miss Cluck was finally calm, she said, "As you know, our forty-second annual Pie Festival is today. And, as I do every year, I made a pie to enter into the pie contest. Last year, I entered my blueberry pie and won second place. Since then I have been improving my recipe. I just know . . . I just feel certain this year is my year to win first place."

From previous years of going to the Pie Festival, Biscuit and Joe-Joe knew well how good Miss Cluck's pies tasted. MMMM, MMMM, Delicious!

"Where was the pie last seen?" asked Joe-Joe.

"It was on the window sill, cooling." Miss Cluck's wing pointed towards her kitchen window. "I left it right there while I cleaned up the kitchen. When I was finished, I turned around to check on the pie—and it was gone!"

Biscuit and Joe-Joe breathed deeply. The aroma of the pie still saturated the air, creating a pleasant fog.

"Joe-Joe, let's check out the window sill," urged Biscuit as he pulled Joe-Joe back out the front door. As they walked around the house to observe the window sill, they noticed four sets of tracks. As each set left, it branched off in four different directions.

"Miss Cluck?" called Biscuit.

Miss Cluck's head poked partially out of the window. "Yes?"

"We found tracks. Have you had any visitors this morning?" inquired Joe-Joe.

"Oh, yes! Several of my friends came to wish me luck. Let's see, there was Phineas Frog, Wiley Q. Duck, Ramona Raccoon, and, of course, my closest friend, Belinda Bear." Miss Cluck paused briefly. "Why?"

"Well, it's possible one of your friends might have taken your pie," concluded Biscuit. "We'll need to follow the evidence to find out the truth, but until then, your four friends are suspects in this case."

Miss Cluck raised her wings and pressed them over her beak. "Oh, no, no, no. None of them would have taken my pie!"

"Would you stake the first place trophy on that, Miss Cluck?" asked Joe-Joe with one eyebrow raised.

Miss Cluck opened her beak and then closed it just as fast. "I see your point. What's next?"

"Joe-Joe and I are going to follow the tracks and see where they lead. After questioning each suspect, we'll then be able to determine which one committed the crime. We should have our answer soon."

"Good! Because the contest begins in just a few hours. I'm depending on the both of you to solve this case and find my pie. Keep me posted!" finished Miss Cluck as she left the window, leaving the problem up to the detectives to solve.

Biscuit took out a measuring tape from his jacket pocket where he kept everything he would ever need inside, and measured the distance from the ground to the window, it measured two feet. Joe-Joe wrote down the measurement on his notepad. Now they knew that the suspect had to have a reach of at least two feet tall in order to grab the pie from the window sill safely, and, given the fact that the pie was a blueberry pie, it would make a very important clue if that particular pie was the thief's favorite. Joe-Joe wrote that information down as well.

Then Biscuit studied the size and length of each track. Though underneath the window the tracks overlapped, when he looked beyond that to the trail each of the suspects followed as they walked away, Biscuit could tell that each was of a different height and weight

depending on the size of it's track and the depth of the impression it made in the dirt. Biscuit began to measure each track. The lengths ranged from one inch up to eleven inches. The suspects also ranged from small to very large in size. The information made sense.

As soon as Biscuit Bill and Joe-Joe gathered the information they needed, Biscuit put the measuring tape back inside of his jacket pocket and took out his magnifying glass. With bill to the ground, he began to follow the tracks with Joe-Joe following behind him.

JOE-JOE AND BISCUIT QUESTION
PHINEAS FROG

2

PHINEAS FROG

 The first tracks that Joe-Joe and Biscuit followed were Phineas Frog's. The tracks led them to a large pond filled with cattails and lily pads. It was a serene place full of bird song. Phineas's home was at the edge of the pond. The tracks led right up to his front door. The house was really unique because Phineas lived in a large red and white mushroom. It appeared sturdy, as far as toadstools go, but was too small for Joe-Joe and Biscuit to enter. Biscuit dropped to his knees and knocked on the door. Joe-Joe crouched down as well. After several minutes, Phineas answered, opening

the door wide, his large eyes timidly peering out at his guests.

"Yes? Can I help you?" croaked the frog.

"Yes, sir. My name is Biscuit Bill. This is my partner, Joe-Joe Nut. We're detectives and are investigating Miss Cluck's missing pie. Do you happen to know anything about it?"

Phineas's eyes grew very large. "Miss Cluck's pie? Miss Cluck's soon-to-be-award-winning blueberry pie?" He violently shook his head so that his big eyes actually wobbled. "That's terrible! She must be beside herself what with the judging coming up in just a few hours!"

The detectives glanced into Phineas's house, but they couldn't see very far because it seemed to be full to bursting with colorful blown-up balloons.

With his notepad out and pencil, Joe-Joe began to ask a few questions. "What are the balloons for, sir?"

Phineas glanced back into his house. "Oh, I'm responsible for the balloons for the festival, and I am terribly late," he croaked.

"We just need a few minutes of your time to ask you a few questions. Then we'll let you get on your way," assured Biscuit smoothly.

"Fair enough. I have nothing to hide. Continue away."

"Thank you, sir," said Joe-Joe. "Were you over at Miss Cluck's this morning?"

"Indeed I was. I hopped over to wish her good luck in the pie contest. She makes the most wonderful pies, but last year she only won second place and was very disappointed. I know she's been working hard to perfect her recipe, so I thought to bring her some good will and inspiration."

"Inspiration, sir?" asked Biscuit curiously.

"Well . . ." croaked frog as he moved his head to the left, then to the right, making sure no one could overhear him. Joe-Joe and Biscuit leaned forward in anticipation.

"Between you and me, I recommended that she add flies to her pie. You know, for extra flavor."

Everyone leaned back. Joe-Joe and Biscuit glanced at Phineas's smiling features and couldn't find the heart to disagree.

"How tall are you?" continued Joe-Joe.

"I'm eight inches tall," replied Phineas proudly.

"And your favorite pie, sir?" asked Joe-Joe, though they could have guessed.

Phineas's eyes grew dreamy and he clasped his rubbery little hands together. "Oh, without doubt, my most favorite pie is moo moo fly mud pie. De-lic-ous!" slurped frog as his sticky tongue reached out and then whipped back into his mouth.

"With our years of experience at being detectives, we know that looks can be deceiving. Would you mind participating in an experiment? It would exclude your being a suspect." Phineas thought for a moment, then agreed.

"Absolutely, detectives, what do you want me to do?" Biscuit reached into his pocket and pulled out a yardstick, something that might have been difficult had this been an ordinary pocket. It wasn't. It was, in fact,

a magic pocket. Though Biscuit's pocket was only two inches by two inches, he could keep some pretty large things in it, like a yardstick. He stood it on the ground, making sure that the numbers could be seen by both Joe-Joe and Phineas. He then reached back into his pocket for a black marker. "Thirty-six inches makes up a yard," he explained, "which is three feet. We only need two feet. There are twelve inches in a foot, so in two feet there are twenty-four inches." Biscuit marked the two-foot line on the yardstick. Biscuit put the marker back into his pocket.

"Miss Cluck's window is two feet high. If Phineas took the pie, he'll be able to jump up to this black line on the yardstick."

Biscuit reached into his magic pocket again, this time pulling out a fly. "To give you inspiration. I'll place this juicy fly on the two foot mark. Ready?"

Phineas glanced up at the black mark and nodded. He then crouched down and jumped with all of his might. Several times Phineas landed on the yardstick, but he couldn't quite jump as high as the black line.

His tongue whipped out several times trying to reach the fly, his eyes bulging with his efforts, but he couldn't do it.

After six tries, Biscuit halted the experiment, putting the yardstick back into his pocket. Phineas was amazed when Biscuit took it out of his pocket, but to see it slowly disappear into the pocket, Phineas's mouth dropped open.

Joe-Joe laughed. "Crazy isn't it?"

Phineas recovered quickly, glancing back into his house at the balloons. They knew he was pressed for time and wanted to be on his way. There were no more reasons to detain him. Joe-Joe and Biscuit glanced at each other and shook their heads.

"Thank you for your time, sir. Do you need help carrying those balloons to the festival?" asked Biscuit.

"Oh, no, detective, I can manage, but thanks for asking." Phineas hopped quickly inside his house and grabbed hold of the strings tied to the balloons. He then hopped past Joe-Joe and Biscuit, who had now risen from the ground, and merrily went on his

way to the festival. Not being able to resist, they watched Phineas hop across a field towards town. A few times the detectives thought that he might fly away with the balloons, for the balloons seemed to have a mind of their own as the wind caught them, but his sticky hands and feet kept him grounded.

JOE-JOE AND BISCUIT QUESTION
WILEY Q. DUCK

3
WILEY Q. DUCK

 The second set of tracks led the detectives to a medium-sized house on the other side of the pond. The house was made of wood and was tall enough for Biscuit and Joe-Joe to walk up to, instead of having to kneel down in front of. It was built partially over the edge of the pond on stilts with one window in front by the door and a few on the side. There was a nice long porch that protected visitors from getting their feet wet. Joe-Joe knocked on the nicely carved wooden door. When it opened, a duck with markers gripped in his wing, stood in the doorway.

"Are you Wiley Q. Duck?" asked Biscuit.

"Yes! How can I help you?"

"My name is Biscuit Bill and this is my partner, Joe-Joe Nut. We're detectives and are investigating Miss Cluck's missing pie. Do you happen to know anything about it?"

Wiley's wide duck bill dropped open in surprise. "Miss Cluck . . . missing . . . oh, no, not her . . . not her blueberry entry for the pie contest!"

"Yes, sir," said Biscuit.

Wiley held a wing to his heart and looked for a moment as if he might faint. "Oh, my goodness. Oh, my goodness. I just saw her this morning and wished her good luck with the pie contest today. I can't believe someone would take her pie!"

"We agree completely, Mr. Duck. However, since you were at the home of Miss Cluck's this very morning, we do need to ask you a few questions," said Joe-Joe.

"Of course, of course. Please, fire away, but I must mention that I'm in a bit of a hurry. You see, I'm responsible for making signs for the festival telling which event is where, and I need to put them up as soon as possible."

"We won't take up too much of your time, sir," said Biscuit as he cleared his throat. "I must ask you, how tall are you?"

"Oh, about two feet tall."

"And what's your favorite pie?" asked Biscuit.

"Oh, let's see. Yes, I'd have to say my most favorite pie is lemon plant meringue. Yup, that's my absolute favorite. YUM! YUM!" answered Wiley as he rubbed his stomach.

Biscuit turned towards Joe-Joe and made sure he wrote the answers down, but couldn't resist saying, "You know, lemon plant meringue is a very good pie, especially with a side of vanila-acorn ice cream." Joe-Joe finished what he was writing, raised one arched eyebrow at his friend, then glanced back over at Wiley.

"Have you ever eaten a blueberry pie, Mr. Duck?"

"Oh, no, detective. I stay away from all berries. I'm allergic so I won't touch them,

though I will admit that Miss Cluck's blueberry pie smelled heavenly."

Joe-Joe quickly scribbled something on his notepad when Wiley continued, "Is that all? I really do need to go."

Biscuit and Joe-Joe glanced quickly at each other, both silently agreeing.

"Of course, sir, we appreciate your time. Do you need some help with those signs?" asked Biscuit. Wiley waddled back into his house, laid the markers on the table, then grabbed the signs with both wings and carried them out the door.

"I've got it, detectives, but thanks for asking." Then Wiley paused for a moment. "Actually, can you get the door?"

"Absolutely!" replied Joe-Joe as he closed Wiley's front door after him. Joe-Joe and Biscuit stood watching as Wiley Q. Duck waddled his way rather heavily through the field towards town.

"Well, another suspect who couldn't have committed the crime," said Joe-Joe. "Phineas is only eight inches tall. There is no way he could have reached high enough to

grab the pie from the window sill . . . or suc-
cessfully land back on the ground without
being squished. Wiley is just tall enough to
have reached the pie, but if he's allergic to
berries, there is no way he would touch it."

"I agree!" said Biscuit. "Shall we move
on to the next suspect?"

"After you, dear friend, but I must say
that all of this talk about pie is starting to
make me hungry." The detectives laughed as
they went back to the main trail and followed
the third set of tracks.

JOE-JOE AND BISCUIT QUESTION
BELINDA BEAR

4

BELINDA BEAR

These tracks were large and led the detectives to Belinda the Brown Bear's den, which was a carved-out large rock. She had created a window to one side, and Joe-Joe and Biscuit could smell something wonderful coming from inside. The aroma caused their stomachs to growl. The door to Belinda's den was quite a bit taller than the other doors they had visited during their investigation that day. Biscuit raised his hand and knocked on the heavy wooden door. The sound seemed to echo. When the door opened, Belinda the Brown Bear loomed over the

very small duck and squirrel. She was wearing an apron covered with flour. She must have been baking up a storm.

"Are you Belinda Bear?" asked Biscuit.

"Yes. How can I help you?"

"Well, I'm Biscuit Bill and this is my partner, Joe-Joe Nut. We're detectives and are investigating a case of a missing pie. Do you happen to know anything about any missing pies?"

Belinda blinked at them, then shrugged her massive shaggy shoulders.

"I can't say that I do. I've been right here at home, spending most of the morning baking my own pie for the pie contest."

"So, you didn't stop by Miss Cluck's house this morning?" asked Joe-Joe suspiciously.

"Oh, yes. I did go over to her house just before I got started with my own baking."

"You said you were here all morning," said Joe-Joe.

"Well, no, I said I was here *most* of the morning. I was, too. But I also went to visit Miss Cluck to wish her good luck for the pie

28

contest. She makes such good pies, and I knew she would be creating a masterpiece this year, especially because I won first place last year. It was just good sportsmanship to wish her luck. She's my biggest rival, but we're such good friends. I understand she's making blueberry pie again, but a new recipe."

"Her pie wasn't made when you stopped by?"

"Oh, no. I stopped by quite early. After all I had my own pie to make. I've been doing that since then."

"Is that your pie there in your paw?" Belinda was holding a wonderful looking pie that caused Joe-Joe's stomach to growl even louder. Belinda raised the pie to her nose and sniffed, her eyes closing. After a moment, she opened her eyes and said, "No, this isn't my pie for the contest. This is my insect-and-root pot pie. It's for my dinner tonight. As I said before, I have been baking all morning. I didn't want to waste left-over dough, so I turned it into the crust for my pot pie."

"Hmmm!" said Joe-Joe as he made some notes. "How tall are you, Miss Bear?"

"Oh, about seven and a half feet," answered Belinda.

"And your favorite pie?" asked Joe-Joe.

"I must say that it's berry pie. My contest entry is a delicious blackberry pie. Would you like to see it?"

If it tasted half as good as it smelled, Joe-Joe and Biscuit knew the contest was going to be close . . . that is if they found Miss Cluck's pie in time for her to compete. Belinda turned around, leaving the detectives at the door, and walked into her kitchen to set the pot pie onto the table. She then turned towards her kitchen window to show to the detectives her contest entry, but stopped and growled, then roared loudly. Joe-Joe and Biscuit ran quickly inside.

"What's wrong? What happened?" they both asked.

"My pie! My pie's *gone*! It was cooling right here on the window sill."

All eyes were on the empty window sill.

"Now we have *two* missing pies?" spouted Joe-Joe.

Biscuit sighed. "I think so. Now, we have two mysteries to solve," he said sadly.

Joe-Joe and Biscuit darted outside to stand underneath the window sill. They were both tall enough to reach the window, but their focus was underneath it pressed into the ground. There were tracks leading from the window towards town. Joe-Joe and Biscuit stared at each other. "The raccoon!"

Raccoon tracks had been under Miss Cluck's window, too. These were the last tracks they had to investigate, the next place they had planned to stop. After whispering back and forth on what they should do, the detectives walked back inside Belinda's den. The expression on her face was not a pleasant one.

"Miss Bear, we think we know who took your pie, and Miss Cluck's. Go get her and meet us at the festival. All will be revealed there."

"What? You think you'll be able to get our pies back?" asked Belinda hopefully.

"We're detectives, Miss Bear, and we always find the truth. Don't worry, your pie is in good hands."

Belinda paused for a moment, then took off her apron, threw it over a kitchen chair and ran out the door.

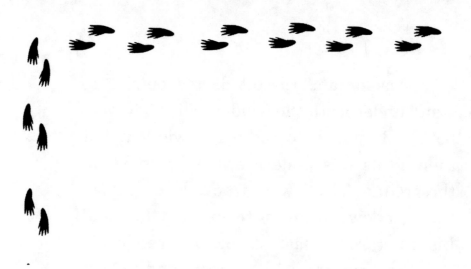

JOE-JOE AND BISCUIT QUESTION
RAMONA RACCOON

5

THE PIE CONTEST

 Biscuit Bill and Joe-Joe Nut were soon on the trail of the raccoon, who had been at both Miss Cluck's house and Belinda Bear's den. The case was getting more complicated by the minute. The raccoon tracks led the detectives to a tree house on Ella Street. They quickly climbed the spiral stairs wrapped around the tree trunk. When they reached the top, and being careful not to fall, Joe-Joe peeked through the nearest oval window. Inside was Ramona Raccoon holding a clipboard. She was making big checks on it as Biscuit knocked on the door. When the door opened, they could see a number of pies sitting on the counter.

"Yes?" spoke Ramona Raccoon.

"Good morning, ma'am. My name's Biscuit Bill, and this is my partner, Joe-Joe Nut. We're investigating some missing pies, and I'm afraid you're our prime suspect in the crime, Miss Ramona. What do you have to say for yourself?"

Ramona held the clipboard to her chest, her eyes wide and bulging.

"Excuse me? Crime? I don't think . . . what? I . . . I'm . . . I'm innocent of any crime! And I most certainly . . . most certainly . . . I did not *steal* any pies!" stuttered Ramona.

"Likely story," began Joe-Joe as he walked into the house and pointed at the pies. "The evidence is right here. You were caught pie handed. That one looks like a blueberry pie, which is what Miss Cluck is missing, and that one . . . yup, that's blackberry, and that's what Belinda Bear is missing."

Ramona stared at the pies on the table. "But that is Miss Cluck's pie, and that blackberry one is indeed Belinda Bear's. I know

what this must look like, but it's a simple misunderstanding, I assure you. I'm the pie contest coordinator for the festival. I sent out letters to all the contestants to have their pies ready by 10:00 this morning, so I can pick them up and have them judged by this afternoon. In the past we had everyone bring in their pies, and that proved to be a problem as some contestants had trouble arranging for their pies to be brought and were either too small or didn't have a way to bring them in. It was Sissy Snake on the committee who helped us understand some of the problems. So, we arranged to pick up the pies this year. Belinda Bear's pie was the last one on my list, and I just picked that one up a few minutes ago."

Biscuit and Joe-Joe stared back and forth at each other in confusion.

"Belinda and Miss Cluck said nothing about receiving a letter," said Biscuit. "When did you send it out?"

"Yesterday! I gave it too . . ." Ramona paused. She sighed and said, "Ohhhh, I know what happened. You see, I gave those letters

to Tristan the Tortoise. He is our mail carrier. Very reliable, but . . . not fast. However, after racing Harriet the Hare yesterday afternoon, he must have been too tired and didn't make it to everyone's house. Or, he was just especially slow, and some might be getting their letter later today. I am so sorry, detectives, for this misunderstanding." Ramona glanced at her watch. "Oh goodness me, I'm going to be late. Would you detectives mind helping me get the pies to the festival to be judged? I have trays over there."

Joe-Joe and Biscuit both looked at the trays, smiled and then glanced at each other. "We would be delighted to help you," said the detectives in unison.

An hour later, the pie judging stage was filled with all sorts of pies. There were apple and banana, cherry and lime, pumpkin and pistachio, and let's not forget, blackberry and blueberry pie. There were also acorn and crab apple, clover and honey, and a white grub and old cheese pie that they carefully set at the end of the table because its "fragrance" was somewhat overpowering. A

crowd had gathered below the stage eagerly awaiting the results.

After helping Ramona with the pies, Biscuit and Joe-Joe found Belinda and Miss Cluck in the crowd. They quietly explained the misunderstanding to the great relief of Miss Cluck and Belinda Bear. Then they brought them up onto the stage to see for themselves that their pies were safe and among the entrants on the tables. They were both relieved. After that they returned to their spots in the crowd to await the judging.

Each member of the crowd watched with interest as the judges seated at a long rectangular table each received a piece of pie to taste. In front of them were scoring sheets, and each of them could be seen writing down their opinion after tasting each pie. The judges tasted pies for almost an hour, then retired to the back of the stage to talk over their choices until a decision was made.

When the head judge, Ramona Raccoon, came forward and stood at a podium, Miss Cluck and Belinda—both very nervous—held each other's paw and wing

and wished each other good luck as Ramona Raccoon waited for quiet so she could announce the winner. She held a microphone in one paw and the results in the other.

"First, I would like to thank all the contestants for participating in our pie contest. I would like to also thank the judges for their time today. After trying each pie, I must say that each one was unique and wonderful in its own way." Ramona paused briefly. "Now, to the results. For the first time ever, we have a tie." The murmurs in the crowd grew louder and louder. "The first place winners of our forty-second annual pie contest are . . . Miss Cluck for her wonderful blueberry pie with its flaky crust and Belinda Bear for her lucious blackberry pie. Both were equally superb."

A roar and wild clucking came up from the crowd as the winners took the stage and received their trophies.

Joe-Joe and Biscuit celebrated the victory—and solving their case—by eating slices of the winning pies awarded to them. Both pies were indeed delicious, and they were

very glad they hadn't had to judge them. As the winners were celebrating, Tristan the Tortoise finally made his slow climb up the stairs and across the stage. When he reached the winners, he handed them each an envelope with the information about the pies being picked up by Ramona, and then continued on his way down the stairs, heading towards home, looking oh so tired.

Belinda and Miss Cluck opened the letters and laughed loudly, while Ramona shook her head and rolled her eyes. Joe-Joe took out his notepad and wrote, "The case of the missing pie is officially CLOSED!" He then returned the notepad to his pocket and congratulated Biscuit on a job well done.

The detectives decided to stay at the festival for the rest of the day to enjoy the festivities. It was indeed a day to remember.

THE END

ANIMAL FACTS AND QUESTIONS

This is a great opportunity to do some research about each animal and find out about what makes each one of them unique and different. There is so much information to be found on-line or in books that you will be amazed. I have some questions to get you started. So have fun and enjoy. Remember to visit my Website at <www.reneeahand.com> for coloring activities and puzzles to enhance your learning.

Which track do you think belongs to each animal?

A)

C)

B)

D)

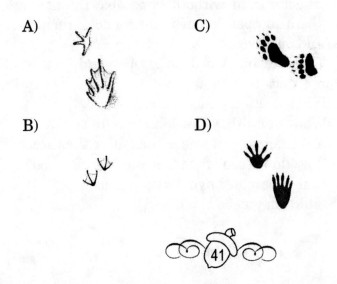

Raccoons

The raccoon has heavy fur streaked in brown, black and gray with a distinctive black face mask that makes him look like a bandit and a bushy ringed tail. Raccoons are nocturnal, so they are most active after dark. They spend the daytime sunbathing or snoozing in trees. The raccoon is an excellent climber and a great swimmer. Contrary to what most people think, it does not wash everything it eats. It is, however, clever  and agile and highly adapted to gathering and eating a great variety of foods. They have been seen in backyards digging up bugs in the grass, and of course, raiding garbage cans. (Ramona would have loved that grub and old cheese pie.) They have five toes on both the front and hind feet, and their front paws look like little hands except they do not have opposable thumbs. Their long, dexterous fingers, even without opposable thumbs, still enable them to open latches, untie knots, turn doorknobs, and open jars.

The raccoon is a deep sleeper and in the fall develops a thick layer of fat to keep warm over winter.

What is a baby raccoon called?

What must they have in order to survive?

Are there any places named after the raccoon?

Why do raccoons wash some of their food?

Can a person have a raccoon as a pet? If so, what would they need?

Frogs

Frogs are amphibians. They are cold blooded, which means their body temperature tends to be the same or close to the temperature of the air around them. That doesn't mean that they can't change their body temperature. To stay cool on a very hot day, they burrow underground or stay under water. To warm up on chilly mornings, they bask in the sun.

Frogs have four legs but no teeth. They do not have ears like a cat or dog, but hear through an organ called a tympanum, which looks like a circle in the skin about where ears might be.

Frogs "talk" or "sing" by pulling air from their lungs into a vocal sac that makes the throat swell out like a balloon. As the air travels past vocal chords, it makes their particular sound, which can be a peeping, sometimes a clucking or almost a booming. The calls they make can be surprisingly loud, even from a very tiny frog.

Because frogs are amphibians, they can live on land and in the water. When they are underwater, they can absorb oxygen through their skin. Even when they are out of the water, their skin is often moist. Some frogs are found in trees and on the screens of houses. They hunt insects there, then return to some moist place or a pond. Most frogs lay their eggs in water.

Frogs can jump longer than the length of their bodies, and, for their size, swim ten times faster than a human.

Frogs go through metamorphosis, which means they change shape as they grow. Frogs start out as an egg that is often part of a jelly-like mass of eggs laid by the mother frog among the weeds in a pond or lake. After they hatch, they look like a minnow and have gills to breathe underwater. At this stage, they have no legs, but do have a tail that looks like the tail of a fish. Then they grow legs and finally lungs so they can live on land. The tail gradually disappears as the legs develop. Adults don't have any tail at all, just the stumpy end of their spine.

What are the stages of a frog's metamorphosis called?

Are there any other animals that also go through metamorphosis?

What is the difference between a frog and a toad?

What is the largest frog in the world, and where is it located?

What is the smallest frog in the world, and where does it live?

Ducks

Ducks are aquatic birds, members of the Anatidae family. They are related to geese and swans but are usually smaller in size compared to them. Ducks can be found in forest wetlands, near rivers, swamps, ponds, and lakes. All the many varieties of domesticated ducks, except muscovies, are descended from mallards which are not native to the United States, but were imported from China. Mallards are probably the most numerous duck on the planet. However, they are just one of many species of ducks.

Ducks have webbed feet. These act like paddles. Ducks provide us with eggs, meat, and feathers. A down comforter or sleeping bag can be stuffed with the soft feathers of certain ducks, which make it very cozy and warm. A male duck is called a drake. A female duck is called a hen. Babies are called ducklings.

Most ducks, though they spend a lot of time on water, don't actually swim. Ducks' feathers are waterproof. A duck sitting on water is floating. So that it floats and paddles with its webbed feet. Ducks spend a lot of time preening its feathers and renewing the waterproofing on them by spreading an oil from a gland near their tails onto the feathers. If ducks, even diving ducks that swim underwater to catch fish, lose this waterproofing, they will drown.

Can ducks be found on both fresh water and sea water?

Many species of duck are temporarily flightless while molting. What is molting? Why would a duck go through molting? And what other animals, birds, insects, and reptiles molt?

What is the difference between a duckling and a chick?

When ducks quack, do they have an echo?

How many eyelids do ducks have?

Are ducks social animals? If so, explain.

Do ducks get cold feet?

Bears

The brown bear (*Ursus arctos*), otherwise known as the grizzly bear is one of the largest North American land mammals and is a symbol of America's wild lands. They live in dense forests in mountains, valleys, and meadows and can be found in Canada, in central regions of the U.S. and throughout Europe and Asia. Brown bears are recognized by their most distinctive feature, their heavy shoulder hump. The United States has one other bear, the black bear.

Super strong shoulder muscles help the brown bear dig up roots and tear apart logs to find food. These muscles are located in the hump of the brown bear. Brown bears can move rocks and logs and dig through hard soil and rocky ground to make their dens or look for food, using their long sharp claws. Bears are called omnivores. They eat grass, fruit, insects, roots, and bulbs of plants along with carrion, and they will hunt small or young animals. Brown bears that live near the coast love fish, particularly salmon. These bears will grow much larger than those living in other areas because of their protein-rich diet.

What other animals are omnivores?

Brown bears have a life span of about twenty-five years in the wild. Male bears are called boars, and female bears are called sows. What are baby bears called?

What are some of the brown bear sub-species? How did the grizzly bear get its name? Look up the scientific name of the grizzly bear. What do the words sound like? Why do you think it got that name? What are some things you can do to help prevent an unhappy encounter with a bear?

Do all bears hibernate? During hibernation, do bears go to the bathroom?

How many different kinds of bears are there?

What is the difference between a carnivore, a herbivore, and an omnivore?

Do bears travel in herds or are they solitary animals?

Answers to the track quiz on page 39:
   A) Frog
   B) Duck
   C) Bear
   D) Raccoon